MISTY COPELAND

GROUNDBREAKING DANCER

by Rachel Rose

Consultant: Beth Gambro
Reading Specialist, Yorkville, Illinois

BEARPORT
PUBLISHING

Minneapolis, Minnesota

Teaching Tips

BEFORE READING

- Look at the cover of the book. Discuss the picture and the title.
- Ask readers to brainstorm a list of what they already know about Misty Copeland, including what they learned from the cover. What can they expect to see in this book?
- Go on a picture walk, looking through the pictures to discuss vocabulary and make predictions about the text.

DURING READING

- Read for purpose. Encourage readers to look for key pieces of information they can expect to see in biographies.
- Ask readers to look for the details in the book. What happened to Misty Copeland at different times of her life?
- If readers encounter an unknown word, ask them to look at the sounds in the word. Then, ask them to look at the rest of the page. Are there any clues to help them understand?

AFTER READING

- Encourage readers to pick a buddy and reread the book together.
- Ask readers to name three things Misty Copeland has done throughout her life. Go back and find the pages that tell about these things.
- Ask readers to write or draw something they learned about Misty Copeland.

Credits:
Cover and title page ©Monica Schipper/Stringer and ©slobo/iStock; 3, ©Jon Kopaloff/Getty Images; 5, ©Naim Chidiac/Wikimedia; 7, ©trekandshoot/Shutterstock; 8, ©Kevin Karzin/AP Images; 11, ©CBS Photo Archive/Getty Images; 13, ©Patrick McMullan/Getty Images; 14, ©MediaNews Group/Orange County Register via Getty Images/Getty Images; 17, ©FOX/Getty Images; 19, ©Bruce Glikas/Getty Images; 21, ©Hiroyuki Ito/Getty Images; 22, ©Earl Gibson III/Getty Images; 23, ©Artur Didyk/Shutterstock; 23, ©A_Lesik/Shutterstock

Library of Congress Cataloging-in-Publication Data

Names: Rose, Rachel, 1968- author.
Title: Misty Copeland : groundbreaking dancer / by Rachel Rose.
Description: Minneapolis, Minnesota : Bearport Publishing Company, [2022] |
Series: Bearcub bios | Includes bibliographical references and index.
Identifiers: LCCN 2020054972 (print) | LCCN 2020054973 (ebook) | ISBN 9781647478445 (library binding) | ISBN 9781647478520 (paperback) | ISBN 9781647478605 (ebook)
Subjects: LCSH: Copeland, Misty--Juvenile literature. | African American ballerinas--Biography--Juvenile literature.
Classification: LCC GV1785.C635 R67 2022 (print) | LCC GV1785.C635 (ebook) | DDC 792.802/8092 [B]--dc23 LC record available at https://lccn.loc.gov/2020054972LC ebook record available at https://lccn.loc.gov/2020054973

Copyright © 2022 Bearport Publishing Company. All rights reserved. No part of this publication may be reproduced in whole or in part, stored in any retrieval system, or transmitted in any form or by any means, electronic, mechanical, photocopying, recording, or otherwise, without written permission from the publisher.

For more information, write to Bearport Publishing, 5357 Penn Avenue South, Minneapolis, MN 55419. Printed in the United States of America.

Contents

Top Dancer 4

Misty's Life 6

Did You Know? 22

Glossary 23

Index 24

Read More 24

Learn More Online 24

About the Author 24

Top Dancer

Misty Copeland jumped across the **stage**.

She had just become a top dancer for ABT.

Misty was the first African American woman to get the job.

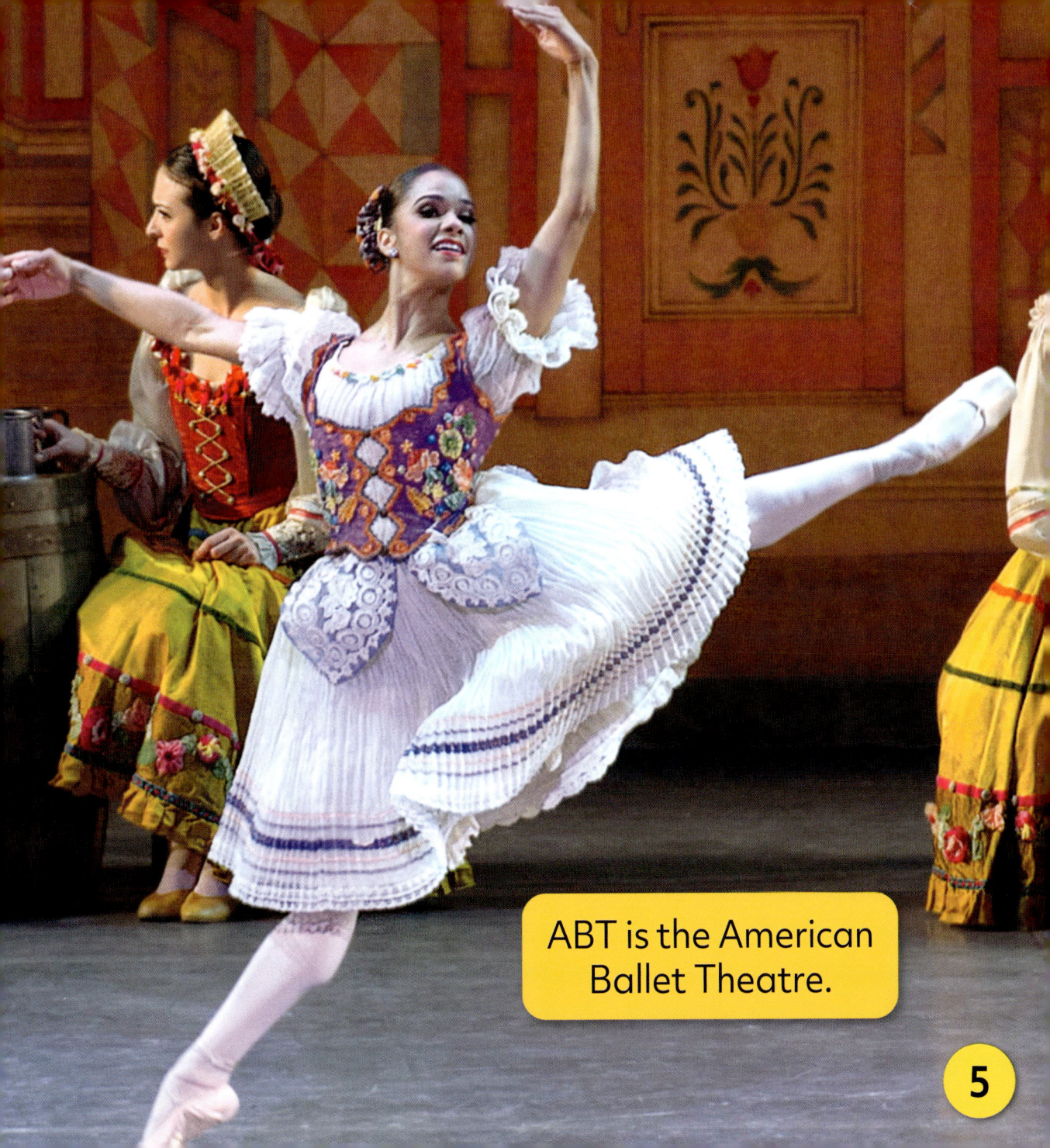

ABT is the American Ballet Theatre.

Misty's Life

Misty was born in Missouri.

Her family moved to California when she was two.

They did not have much money.

Life was hard sometimes.

When she was 13, Misty started dancing **ballet**.

It was a very late start for a dancer!

But dance made Misty happy.

Misty danced very well.

She worked hard.

Misty started dancing for ABT when she was 18.

It is one of the best ballet **companies**.

Misty stood out.

She did not look like other dancers at ABT.

But Misty was great at ballet.

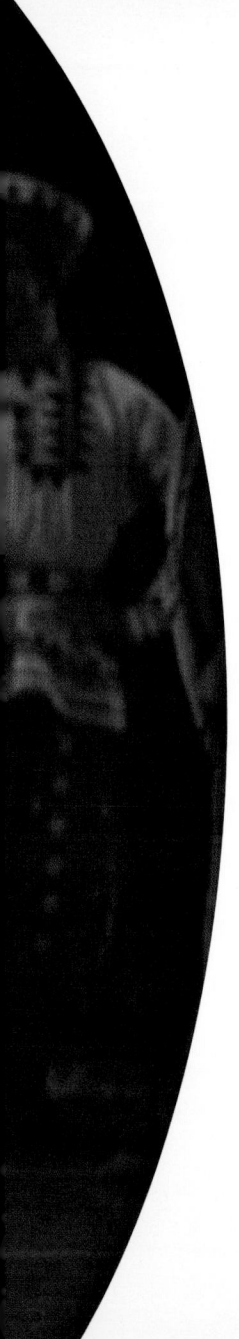

She danced so well that she got big parts.

Then, Misty was made a top dancer.

It was her dream come true!

Misty wanted to help others like her.

She told her story in books.

She was a **judge** on a TV show for dancers.

Misty likes to work with young dancers.

She helps the Boys and Girls Clubs of America.

It is where she first learned to dance.

Misty wants to show everyone what she has done.

She wants young girls to know they can be anything.

Did You Know?

Born: September 10, 1982

Family: Sylvia (mother), Doug (father), Erica (sister), Douglas Jr. (brother), Christopher (brother), Cameron (brother), Lindsay (sister)

When she was a kid: Misty lived with her ballet teacher for a while.

Special fact: There is a doll that was made to look just like Misty.

Misty says: "Finding ballet was like finding the missing piece in myself."

Life Connections

Misty wanted to do something nobody like her had ever done. What is something you want to do that has not been done before?

Glossary

ABT a ballet company in New York

ballet a kind of dance

companies groups of people who come together to do things, such as dance

judge a person who decides in a contest

stage a place where people act, dance, or sing

23

Index

ballet 9–10, 12, 22
books 16
Boys and Girls Clubs 18
California 6–7
dance 9, 18
judge 16
Missouri 6

Read More

Howden, Sarah. *Misty Copeland: Ballet Star (I Can Read! Level 1).* New York: HarperCollins, 2020.

Sarantou, Katlin. *Misty Copeland (My Itty-Bitty Bio).* Ann Arbor, MI: Cherry Lake, 2020.

Learn More Online

1. Go to **www.factsurfer.com**
2. Enter "**Misty Copeland**" into the search box.
3. Click on the cover of this book to see a list of websites.

About the Author

Rachel Rose is a writer who lives in San Francisco. Her favorite books to write are those about people who lead inspiring lives.